The Marching Band

by Frances Ann Ladd

Illustrated by Duendes del Sur

D0888269

SCHOLASTIC INC.

New York   Toronto   London   Auckland   Sydney
Mexico City   New Delhi   Hong Kong   Buenos Aires

Shaggy and Scooby
were at school.
They were new
in the band.
Shaggy had a tuba.
Scooby had a drum.
"I love being in the band!"
said Shaggy.

The bandleader shouted,
"Line up!"
Shaggy and Scooby
lined up.
"March!"
The band started
to march.

First they marched
straight.
"Turn left!"
The band turned left.
But Scooby turned right!
Bam!
Then the band
turned right.
Scooby turned left.
Wham!

"Play!"
The band started to play.
Shaggy tooted
on the tuba.
Scooby banged
on the drum.
"Louder!"
The band played louder.
"Softer!"
The band played softer.

"Stop!"
Everyone stopped.
But Scooby and Shaggy
played on.
*Oompa, oompa,
boom-boom-boom!*
They were having
too much fun!

"You two!
Stop playing!"
Shaggy and Scooby
stopped.
"Do you know
how to march and play?"
said the bandleader.
"Like, yeah!"
said Shaggy.
Boom-boom!
Scooby banged
on his drum.
"See?" said Shaggy.

Oops!
Scooby hit the leader
with his drumstick.
"Come here.
I think I have
a good part
for you to play,"
said the leader.

"Like, wow!" said Shaggy.
"Snack duty!
I love being in the band!"

No part of this publication may be reproduced in whole or in part,
or stored in a retrieval system, or transmitted in any form or by any means,
electronic, mechanical, photocopying, recording, or otherwise, without written
permission of the publisher. For information regarding permission, write to
Scholastic Inc., Attention: Permissions Department,
557 Broadway, New York, NY 10012.

ISBN 0-439-67785-8

Copyright © 2004 Hanna-Barbera.
SCOOBY-DOO and all related characters and elements
are trademarks of and © Hanna-Barbera.
CARTOON NETWORK and logo are trademarks of and © Cartoon Network.
All rights reserved.
Used under license by Scholastic Inc. Published by Scholastic Inc.
SCHOLASTIC and associated logos are trademarks
and/or registered trademarks of Scholastic Inc.

Designed by Joan Moloney

28 27 26 25 24 23   13 14

Printed in China   62
First printing, September 2004

Zoinks!

What happens when Scooby and Shaggy join the band?

Read this story to find out and learn all about the "-ed" sounds.

SCHOLASTIC

www.scholastic.com   SCUS 1723

ISBN 0-439-67785-8

50000

9 780439 677851

EAN

Copyright © 2004 Hanna-Barbera.
SCOOBY-DOO and all related characters and elements are trademarks
of and © Hanna-Barbera.
CARTOON NETWORK and logo are trademarks of and © Cartoon Network.
WB SHIELD: TM & © Warner Bros. Entertainment Inc.
(s04)

CARTOON
NETWORK.c

CARTOON
NETWORK
SCOOBY-DOO!

A Whiff of Pizza

SCHOLASTIC

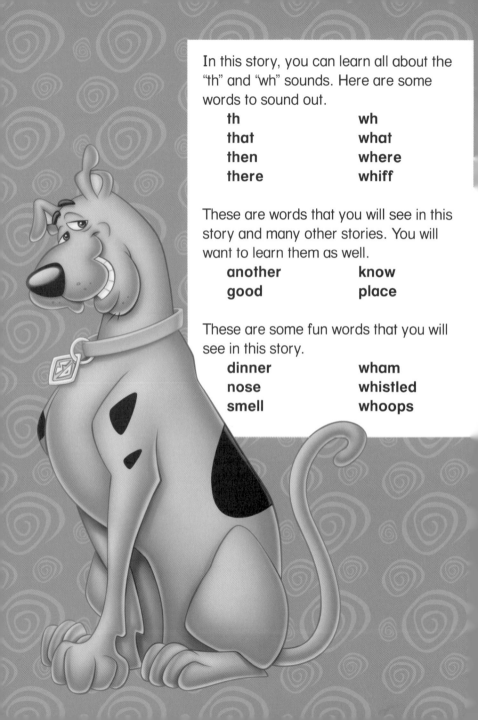

In this story, you can learn all about the "th" and "wh" sounds. Here are some words to sound out.

th	**wh**
that	**what**
then	**where**
there	**whiff**

These are words that you will see in this story and many other stories. You will want to learn them as well.

another	**know**
good	**place**

These are some fun words that you will see in this story.

dinner	**wham**
nose	**whistled**
smell	**whoops**